Circle

Square

Greenwillow Books, *An Imprint of* HarperCollins *Publishers*

Tr Moose

By Kelly Bingham

Pictures by Paul O. Zelinsky

For Marty, my ♡—K. B.

To my family of squares—P. O. Z.

Circle, Square, Moose
Text copyright © 2014 by Kelly Bingham
Illustrations copyright © 2014 by Paul O. Zelinsky
All rights reserved. Manufactured in China.
For information address HarperCollins Children's Books,
a division of HarperCollins Publishers,
195 Broadway, New York, NY 10007.
www.harpercollinschildrens.com

Mixed media were used to prepare the full-color art.
The text type is Geometric 212 Book.

Library of Congress Cataloging-in-Publication Data

Bingham, Kelly L., (date)
Circle, square, Moose / by Kelly Bingham ; pictures by Paul O. Zelinsky.
  pages cm
"Greenwillow Books."
Summary: When Zebra and his enthusiastic friend Moose are asked
to exit a book about shapes, Moose has other plans.
ISBN 978-0-06-229003-8 (trade ed.)—ISBN 978-0-06-229004-5 (library bdg.)
[1. Shape—Fiction. 2. Moose—Fiction. 3. Zebras—Fiction.
4. Behavior—Fiction. 5. Friendship—Fiction.
6. Humorous stories.] I. Zelinsky, Paul O., illustrator II. Title.
PZ7.B51181685Ci 2014 [E]—dc23 2013019534

14 15 16 17 18 SCP 10 9 8 7 6 5 4 3 2 1
First Edition

 Greenwillow Books

Shapes

are all around us. We see them every day. Have you ever looked at a button?

This one is a . . .

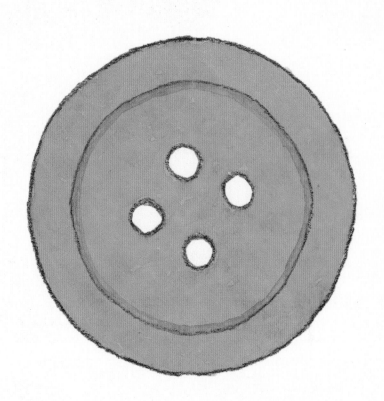

circle.

What
about
that
sandwich
you had
for lunch?

That is a . . .

square.

And if you look closely at a square [...] will see that it is made of four equ[...]

Look—this is a book about shapes. Not animals. You are in the wrong book.

And please put that sandwich back. It's our square.

Now, let's learn about

triangles.

Do you know what a triangle is?

A **TRIANGLE** is . . .

A wedge of cheese

A piece of pie

Cute, but this is not an animal book. It is a shape book. You both need to leave.

Let's talk about rectangles!

A

RECTANGLE

is . . .

A domino

A book

A chocolate bar

he blade of a hoe

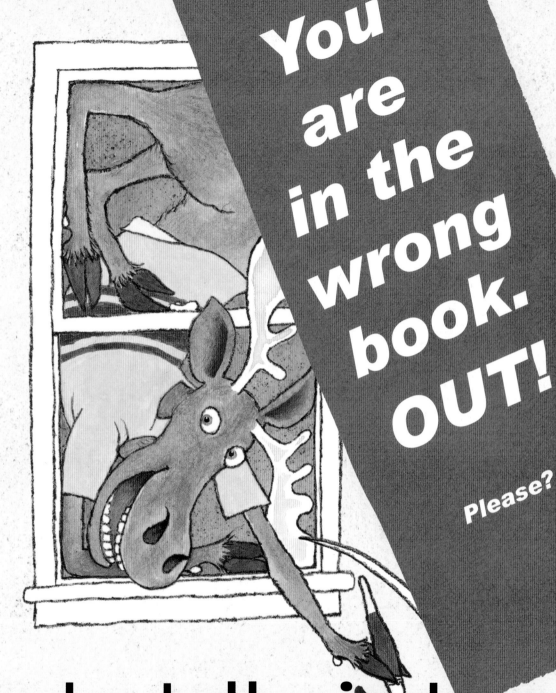

You are in the wrong book. OUT!

Please?

to read   And a tall window

Moose   Hello!

A **DIAMOND** is . . .
The shape in a crown

A flying kite

Okay. You have to leave. You are ruining the book. This is a book about shap

I'll handle this.

A **SQUARE** is . . .

A pretty picture frame

Come back here!

A shiny tile

Or a fun board game

What
is a
curve?
A

CURVE

might

be . . .

A snake-ity snake

A yo-yo

trick

Or a ribbon's wake

A CIRCLE IS ROUND.

A **CIRCLE** is . . .

A polka dot

Help!

A STAR

is for Zebra,
my very good friend.

Zebra and Moose.
Friends
to the
end.